Berry
Bramble

Lilac
Grove

Flower
Garden

D1060334

THE HIDDEN RAINBOW

Christie Matheson

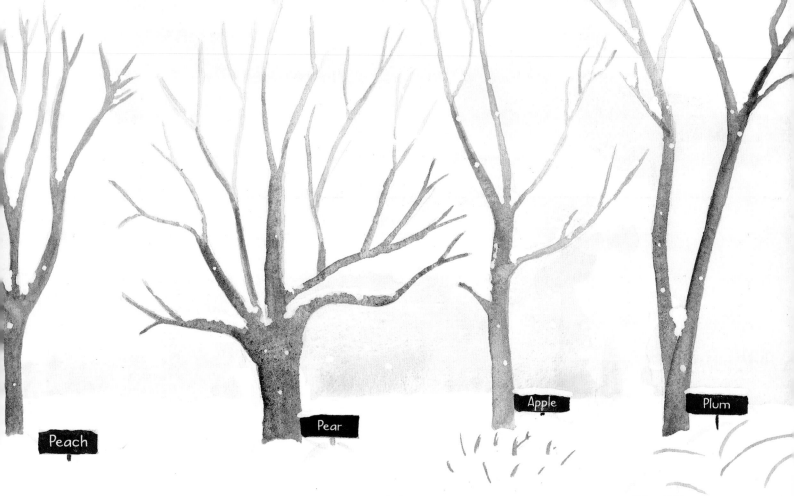

Peach

Pear

Apple

Plum

Greenwillow Books

An Imprint of HarperCollinsPublishers

One little bee peeks out to see
a world of gray and snow.
She's looking for bright colors.
And she needs *you* to help them grow.

First, please brush the snow
off the budding camellia trees.

Camellia

Tulip

Look! The flowers are RED—
and their nectar feeds two bees!

Tickle the very tops
of the growing tulip leaves.

Very soon, the bees will find . . .

ORANGE!
And can you see three bees?

Next, point to the crocus shoots,
just beginning to sprout.

Crocus

Clover

Four bees are eating pollen
now that YELLOW has come out.

Now it's time to search
for a special four-leaf clover.

What luck!
A field of GREEN,
with five bees zooming over.

Please wave the bees back to their hive—
clouds are gathering for a shower.

The bees don't like the rain,
but it's important for the flowers.

Forget-Me-Not

Blow the forget-me-not buds dry

as the rain clears from the sky.

Hyacinth

The sun is shining, BLUE is blooming,
and six bees are buzzing by!

Next, trace a line straight down
the orderly hyacinth row.

Seven bees are foraging
in blooms of INDIGO.

You're practically done!
Now blow a kiss
to the lovely lilac trees.

Lilac

The VIOLET blossoms are brimming
with nectar for eight bees.

At last, get ready to find . . .

nine bees on the RAINBOW you grew!

But the story is not over—
these bees have work to do.

Can you see ten humming bees
getting busy in these trees?

Apple

Peach

They're spreading so much pollen,
you just might have to . . .

Pear

Apple

Plum

Blueberry

Blackberry

Achoo!

And *why* are the bees spreading pollen?
So something *you* eat can grow.

Thanks to the bees, soon you'll have . . .

your own delicious

RAINBOW!

Pear

Apple

Plum

Blueberry

Blackberry

BUSY BEES

During the winter, honeybees stay in their hives and snuggle close to keep warm. They also feed on stored honey and pollen. But by the time spring comes, the food in their hive may be gone and they are hungry!

What do they want to eat? Nectar and pollen from flowers! In many places, camellia trees are some of the first plants to bloom and feed bees. Spring flowers such as tulips, crocuses, clover, hyacinths, and forget-me-nots are also important food sources. Bees also feast on fragrant lilac flowers when they blossom.

Bees get food from a rainbow of flower colors, as long as the flowers offer the nectar and pollen they love to eat—bees' favorite colors in the floral rainbow are yellow, blue, indigo, and violet. They also like white flowers.

You can help bees by planting flowers that feed them. In addition to the flowers in this book, bees love dandelions, snowdrops, bee balm, snapdragons, lavender, sunflowers, poppies, and many others.

Why would you want to help feed bees? Buzzing bees may be small, but they are one of the most important animals on the planet! They are pollinators, which means they move pollen from one part of a plant to another, or from one plant to another.

Thanks to pollination, plants can grow fruits and seeds. Most of the plants we eat need pollination to make fruit and to keep growing year after year. (So do most of the beautiful wildflowers we see.) Scientists say that about one-third of the food we eat relies on pollinators—mainly bees—to grow. Every apple, blueberry, blackberry, peach, pear, and plum you eat was pollinated!

So, next time you see a bee, take a look at where it's buzzing. It just might be pollinating your next delicious treat.

FOR HUNTER AND CHLOE

The Hidden Rainbow
Copyright © 2020 by Christie Matheson.
All rights reserved. Manufactured in China.
For information address HarperCollins Children's Books,
a division of HarperCollins Publishers, 195 Broadway, New York, NY 10007.
www.harpercollinschildrens.com

Watercolor paints and collages were used to prepare the full-color art.
The text type is 30-point Venetian 301 BT.

Library of Congress Cataloging-in-Publication Data

Names: Matheson, Christie, author.
Title: The hidden rainbow / by Christie Matheson.
Description: First edition. | New York : Greenwillow Books, an imprint of HarperCollinsPublishers, [2020] |
Audience: Ages 4-8. | Audience: Grades K-1. | Summary: Illustrations and simple,
rhyming text invite the reader to uncover the rainbow of colors hidden in a garden,
which helps flowers bloom and bees find food. Includes facts about bees and their importance.
Identifiers: LCCN 2019054685 | ISBN 9780062393418 (hardcover)
Subjects: CYAC: Stories in rhyme. | Gardens—Fiction. | Colors—Fiction. | Bees—Fiction.
Classification: LCC PZ8.3.M4227 Hid 2020 | DDC [E]—dc23
LC record available at https://lccn.loc.gov/2019054685

First Edition

20 21 22 23 24 SCP 10 9 8 7 6 5 4 3 2 1

GREENWILLOW BOOKS